Ollie & Moon

in NEW YORK CITY

Diane Kredensor

with photographs by
Mike Meskin

A Random House PICTUREBACK® Book

Random House 🏠 New York

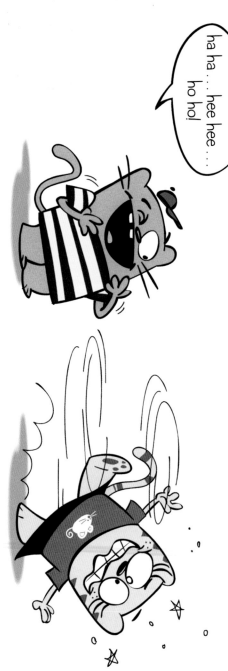

Ollie and Moon are best friends.

Ollie likes to laugh . . . a lot.

And a lot makes him laugh—especially Moon!

Like when she spins in circles until she gets dizzy—

or when she and their friend Stanley compete
in their Funny Lip-Sound Contest.

ha ha . . . hee hee
ho ho!

BBLLBBLLBBLL . . .
BBLLBBLLBBLL . . .

hee hee . . . ho
ho . . . ha ha!
snort!

Moon loves when Ollie laughs, more than anything in the world. So when Moon joined Ollie on the ferry wearing the goofy hat she'd just bought, she was expecting a big laugh from him.

But Ollie didn't even chuckle.

"What's wrong, Ollie?" asked Moon.

"Nothing," he said.

"Why aren't you laughing at my hat?" she said. "It's funny!"

"Sure, it's funny, but it's not *that* funny," Ollie said.

Manhattan

Statue of Liberty
Ellis Island

"I bet I can make you laugh," said Moon.
"I bet you can't," said Ollie.

A handshake sealed the bet. Moon was determined to make Ollie laugh.
"I have an idea," she said. "Follow me!" And off they went.

On the street, they walked by some food vendors. Moon searched carefully. "Dumplings, fish balls, chow mein fun . . . Aha! Perfect!" Moon found what she was looking for. She held up two fingers to the vendor.

Ollie cracked a smile, but he didn't laugh at Moon's gags.

"Hmmm, making you laugh and winning this bet is going to be harder than I thought," said Moon as they headed for the subway.

Musicians were performing on the subway platform. Moon tapped her foot and Ollie worked his dance moves. Moon never danced. She was too embarrassed by her pigeon toes. *But now's my chance to make him laugh!* she thought.

"Hey," said Moon. "Watch this!" And she tried out a few silly moves of her own.

Ollie smiled and cheered Moon on, but he didn't laugh. So they boarded the train and headed uptown.

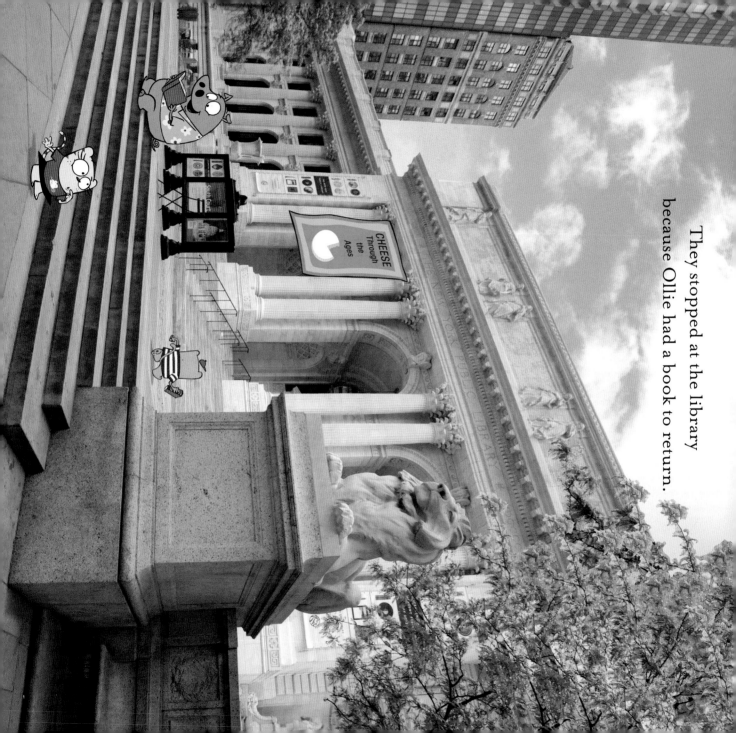

They stopped at the library because Ollie had a book to return.

Moon seized the opportunity to try out her lion-tamer imitation.

Moon thought she was pretty funny.
But Ollie didn't laugh.
Moon wasn't ready to give up, so they went on their way.

Moon hailed a cab.

"Stanley?" asked Ollie.

"No, I'm his cousin Johnny," replied the snail cabdriver.

"Oh, sorry," said Ollie.

"Fuhgeddaboudit," replied Johnny, and then he added a funny lip sound:
"BBLLBBLLBBLLBBLLBBLL . . ."

It was the same sound that Stanley made! Moon joined in, hoping

Ollie would laugh, but he didn't. He just smiled politely.

Moon had an idea that was sure to work.

"First stop, Forty-Second and Broadway, please!" she said.

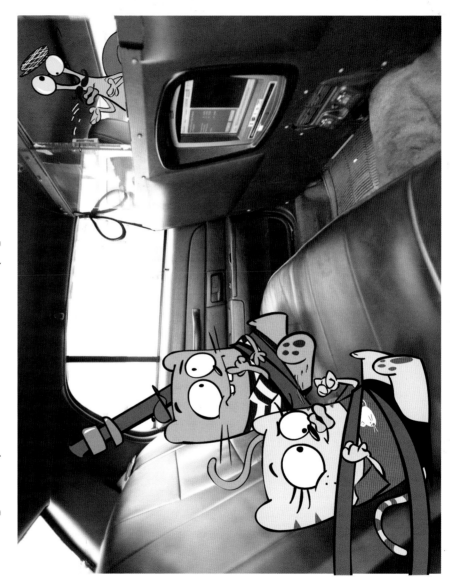

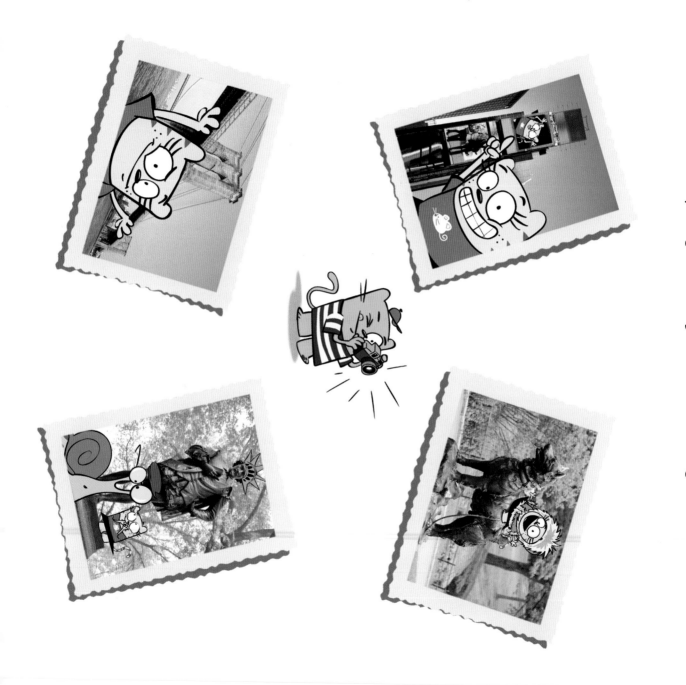

Silly snapshots *always* made Ollie laugh!

But not this time.

So Moon decided to call in the professionals!

But the mimes didn't make Ollie laugh either.

"That's it!" Moon huffed. "I've tried everything I can think of to make you laugh—

a goofy hat,

hot dogs sticking out of my ears,

pigeon-toed dance moves,

my Siegfried and Roy imitation,

silly snapshots. . . .

And I can't believe Johnny's funny lip sounds

or pantomiming chickens didn't make you laugh!

I give up, Ollie. You win."

Ollie started to giggle. "Ha ha . . . ho ho . . . hee hee . . ."

Moon joined in. "Snicker . . . ho ho . . . hee hee . . . ha ha . . ."

They both laughed louder. "HEE HEE . . . HA HA . . . HO HO . . . SNORT!"

And louder. "HO HO . . . AHA HA . . . HEE HEE HEE . . . SNORT!"

They laughed until there were tears in their eyes and their bellies hurt.

"BWAAAHAHAHAHAHA . . . SNORT!!!!!"

"Thanks, Moon. You win!" said Ollie. "Now, *that was funny!*"

Moon was so very happy to see Ollie laugh, even if it had taken all day. She loved his laugh more than anything in the world.

And Ollie loved Moon's laugh just as much!

THE END

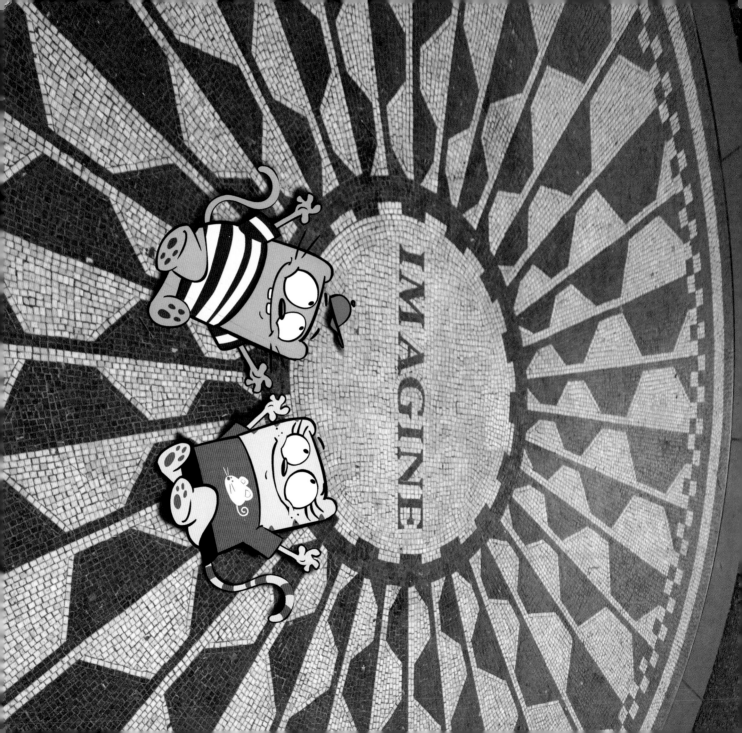

To our little peanut
—D.K.

Picturebook, Random House, and the Random House colophon are
registered trademarks of Penguin Random House LLC.
Sprout and the Sprout logo are registered trademarks of
Children's Network, LLC. All rights reserved.

Visit us on the Web! randomhousekids.com

Educators and librarians, for a variety of teaching tools, visit us at RHTeachersLibrarians.com

The Library of Congress has cataloged the hardcover edition of this book as follows:
Kredensor, Diane.
Ollie & Moon : fuhgeddaboudit! / by Diane Kredensor : photographer, Mike Meskin. — 1st ed.
p. cm.
Summary: Two feline best friends travel to New York City,
where Moon bets Ollie that she can make him laugh.
ISBN 978-0-375-87014-9 (trade) — ISBN 978-0-375-97014-6 (lib. bdg.) —
ISBN 978-0-375-98757-1 (ebook)
[1. Cats—Fiction. 2. Laughter—Fiction. 3. Best friends—Fiction. 4. Friendship—Fiction.
5. New York (N.Y.)—Fiction.] I. Meskin, Mike, ill. II. Title. III. Title: Ollie and Moon. IV. Title: Fuhgeddaboudit!
PZ7.K877On 2012 [E]—dc22 201100475

ISBN 978-1-5247-1574-8 (pbk.)

MANUFACTURED IN CHINA
10 9 8 7 6 5 4 3 2 1

Random House Children's Books supports the First Amendment and celebrates the right to read.

Acknowledgments
The author-illustrator and photographer would like to thank Brooklyn Farmacy &
Soda Fountain in Carroll Gardens, Brooklyn, for the use of their shoppe.